Where Are You, Wilbert?

Bárður Oskarsson
Translated by Marita Thomsen

Owlkids Books

"One, two, three..."

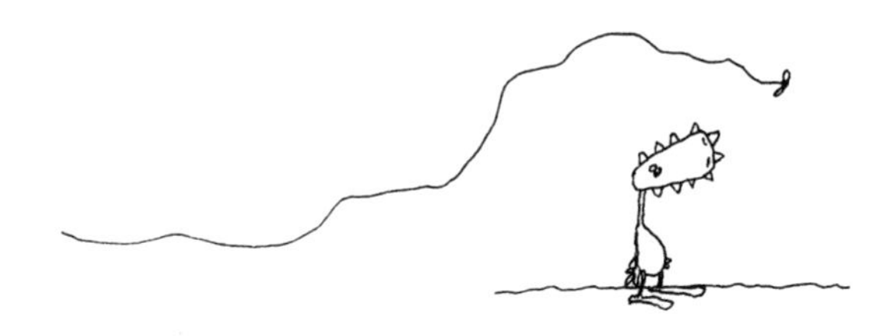

“Ready or not, here I come!”

. . .

• • •

"Hi," said the rat to the crocodile. "I'm looking for my friend Wilbert. Have you seen him?"

"No..." said the crocodile.

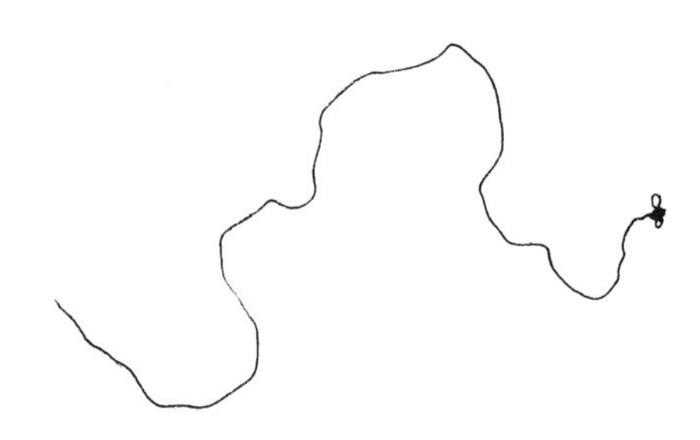

"If you tell me what he looks like, maybe I can help you," said the crocodile.

"Well, he looks a lot like me, only a bit taller."

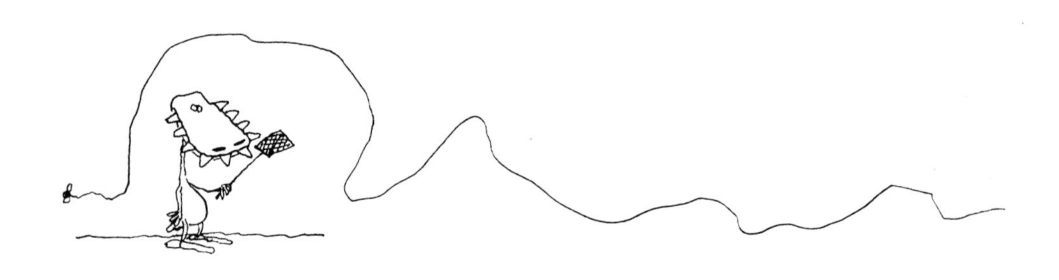

“Oh, him. Sure, I saw him. Actually, I ate him!” said the crocodile.

“OH, NOOOOO!!!!” yelled the rat. She felt scared and sad and angry, all at the same time.

“Ha, ha!” laughed the crocodile. “Got you!
I didn’t eat him, silly.”

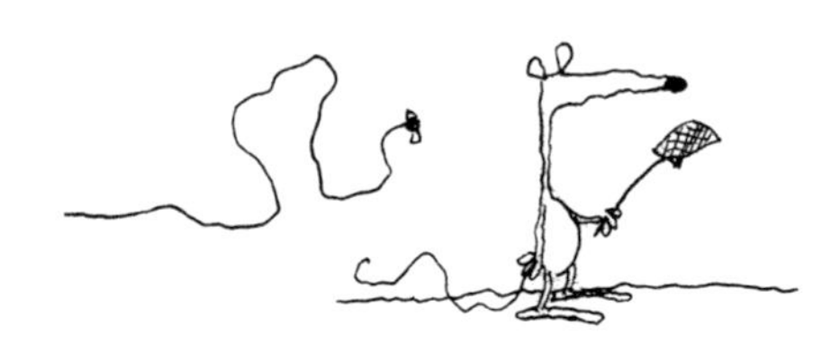

“See?” said the crocodile. “I haven’t eaten anyone.”

"But I can help you look for him. Let's go see if he's hiding over there."

They looked behind every tree they could see,
but there was no Wilbert.

"There he is!" whispered the rat loudly. "Over there, behind that big tree."

The crocodile looked long and hard at the tree and then she looked around the tree, but she couldn't see any sign of Wilbert.

"I can't see him," she said. "Where is he?"

"Hey, Wilbert!" the rat shouted. "I can see you! You're it!"

Then the rat asked the crocodile, "Can you see Wilbert's ears?"

"No," said the crocodile.

"Hey, Wilbert, a crocodile helped me, and we found you," said the rat.

But the crocodile still couldn't see anyone.

She asked the rat, "Is Wilbert still standing over there?"

"No, no," said the rat. "Now he's right here."

After chatting for a while, the rat and Wilbert went back to playing hide-and-seek. They let the crocodile play too.

But even though the crocodile found the rat
every time, she could never find Wilbert.

Published in 2017 by Owlkids Books Inc.

Published in the Faroe Islands under the title *Wilbert* in 2016 by BFL, Faroe Islands,
www.bfl.fo

Owlkids Books acknowledges the financial support of the Canada Council for the Arts, the Ontario Arts Council, the Government of Canada through the Canada Book Fund (CBF) and the Government of Ontario through the Ontario Media Development Corporation's Book Initiative for our publishing activities.

Published in Canada by
Owlkids Books Inc.
10 Lower Spadina Avenue
Toronto, ON M5V 2Z2

Published in the United States by
Owlkids Books Inc.
1700 Fourth Street
Berkeley, CA 94710

Library and Archives Canada Cataloguing in Publication

Oskarsson, Bárður, 1972- [Wilbert. English]
Where are you, Wilbert / Bárður Oskarsson.

Translation of: Wilbert. Translated by Marita Thomsen.
ISBN 978-1-77147-301-9 (hardcover)

I. Thomsen, Marita, translator II. Title. III. Title: Wilbert. English.

PZ7.O825Whe 2017 j839'.6993 C2017-900010-1

Funded by the Government of Canada
Financé par le gouvernement du Canada | Canada

Library of Congress Control Number: 2016962525

Manufactured in Dongguan, China, in April 2017, by Toppan Leefung Packaging & Printing (Dongguan) Co., Ltd.
Job #BAYDC39

A B C D E F

Owlkids Books is a division of